Invitation

When the hottest babe in my senior High school gave me an invitation to a party at the most popular girl in our school's house. First, I was in shock then I accepted without thinking about it.

For the record, the hottest babe in my senior high school is Ashley. The most popular girl in terms of status is Amanda. I accepted the invitation and went back into the house. I went to my room and sat on my bed.

For some reason, I became very nervous. We all live in the upper eastside of Manhattan, New York and go to an elite preparatory school. After an hour, I went to my white mommy Amber's room.

I said look what Ashley next door gave me today. Amber said wow an invitation to a party, how cool. I said I'm nervous, I've never been to one of these parties before nor have I gotten an invite to one before in my entire 4 years at this school.

Amber said its ok, nothing to be nervous about, it's just a party and she hugged me tight and kissed me on the head. I said your right, I'll just go and have fun.

The night of the party, I went into my walking closet and picked out a white collared shirt and black pants, a classic look that never goes out of style.

I put on some cologne and I put on two gold Rolexes on each wrist. I wanted to make a statement at my first party. Amber came in as I was getting ready. She said you look so handsome as I finished getting ready. She said wait I want to take a picture.

Amber took out her phone and took a thousand pictures of me. She said selfie time and took one of both of us. I put my phone and wallet in my pants. Amber called for the car to be ready. Ten minutes later the car was ready and a text was sent to my phone and Amber's phone.

Amber hugged me tight and said have fun. I left and walked to the elevator. I went down to the garage. The car was waiting, I climbed in as the driver held the door. I gave him the address and he took me straight there. I got out of the car and went into the party.

Ashley was already there, I said hello to her and she hugged me tight. A hug from the hottest girl in the school at the party with everyone watching wow.

We talked for a while then the place got hopping like I've seen at night clubs on television. Ashley asked if I wanted to dance. I replied of course, I would love to dance with you.

Ashley and I started dancing and wow she was really grinding on me. I thought this must be some kind of dream. Then I thought oh crap don't get hard, don't get hard. Five minutes later, I was hard as shit.

Ashley felt my hard cock grinding on her pussy and said someone is horny. I said sorry about that Ashley. She said its ok boys get hard and girls get wet. We both laughed out loud.

Ashley held me tight and said oh my god this feels so fucking good, you have no idea baby. I said tell me about it.

Ashley shocked the hell out of me, held my face and kissed me. I went with it and kissed her back but my body was overwhelmed with lustful adrenaline. We kissed for a while massaging each other's tongues.

Ashley said do you want to go to a room where we can be alone. I said sure. Ashley took me by the hand and led me to a room. She locked the door and said so we won't be disturbed.

Ashley pushed me on the bed and I sat down. She took my pants off then my boxers. Ashley said wow that is a big fucking cock. I said thanks, she knelt before me and began licking my cockhead.

Ashley put my cock in her mouth and started sucking my black cock. I held her blonde hair and she blew my mind with pleasure. I couldn't believe hot Ashley next door was sucking my cock.

Ashley stopped and said your turn, she took her red panties off, jumped on the bed and pulled her dress up. I crawled between her sweet white thighs and started licking her pink slit.

I pushed my middle finger inside of Ashley and she moaned then I started chewing on her clit, it drove her wild with passion. She held my head lovingly to her pussy. I thought wow I'm eating the hottest babe in high school, fuck yeah.

Ashley said that's enough of that, time to fuck me with your big black cock. I stopped eating Ashley hopped up on my knees held my dick and pushed my cockhead into her white vagina.

I got the tip in but that was it so I held Ashley's hips and forced the rest of my black penis into her white vagina. I almost died of pleasure sliding balls deep into hot Ashley.

Ashley said damn you have a really big cock. I started sliding my black penis in and out of Ashley's warm vagina.

We both started moaning as we enjoyed our holy union.

Ashley said oh yeah big boy, give it to me, fuck this white girl good black boy. I started fucking her harder and she moaned oh god yes right there. I saw cream on my cock and I thought yeah bitches. I made the hottest babe in my high school cream my fucking dick.

I said bend over Ashley I want you doggie. Ashely said oh yeah, my favorite position. She twerked her big ass and I pushed my black cock back inside of her white pussy.

I held her hips and I started pumping. I heard that

beautiful sound of our skin smacking together and a hard dick inside of a wet pussy. Ashley said oh my god so good as I fucked her harder and harder.

She screamed and creamed the hell out of my cock again. I smacked her ass, pulled her hair and fucked the shit out of her. Ashley said oh yeah big daddy, fill me up baby.

A few moments later, I moaned and threw my head back as an orgasm washed over my entire body. I release my warm sperm, ejaculating all of it into hot Ashley's tight little pink pussy.

I said damn that was hot. Ashley said wow you really

know how to work my white pussy with your big black cock. I said thank you and it was my pleasure to fuck you Ashley. She said it was my pleasure to take your big black pole.

Ashley turned around and we kissed. I grabbed her ass and squeezed. She moaned in my mouth and I said I've always wanted to grab your perfect ass. She said thank you baby. We cuddled and kissed for a little while then Ashley said we better get back to the party before people come looking for us.

We put our discarded clothes back on and went back to the party like nothing happened. I lost track of Ashley in the crowd because she was moving too fast ahead of me.

Amanda grabbed me and said hey I want to show you something. I said ok, she showed me a tape of me fucking Ashley. She said you can agree to be my boyfriend or I'll release this tape to everyone at this party.

I said you know I can't do that to Ashley. Amanda said very well then, she released the video to everyone at the party. I thought oh crap Ashley is going to kill me.

I left the party immediately and went home. I didn't see Ashley one on one for a week. I saw her at school but never close enough to say hello.

A few weeks later, I saw Ashley next door. She said hey are you mad at me. I said no, she said have you seen our sex tape. I said yeah, it's my fault.

Amanda said I had to become her boyfriend or she would release the tape. I told her you know I can't do that to Ashley. She said that fucking bitch. I laughed out loud. Ashley said let's talk on a walk. So, we went for a walk. I said I'm very happy that you're not mad at me.

Ashley said it's not your fault that Amanda is a scheming bitch. I said on the bright side, I made love to the hottest babe in the school. Ashley said whatever, there is plenty of hot babes at our senior high school in case you didn't notice.

I said I've noticed but in my humble opinion, you are the hottest. Ashley said you are only saying that because you fucked me with your huge cock. I said no, I had that opinion before I fucked you.

Ashley's eyes doubled in size and said you are into me. I said hell yeah. Ashley said the feeling is mutual but I wasn't sure until you got hard at the party.

I said for the record, you started grinding on me. I tried to be cool but my passion for you took over.

Ashley said that was the best sex I've ever had with a guy.

I said really wow thank you and for the record that was the best sex I've had with a goddess. Ashley laughed out loud then said are we together as a couple or are we fuck buddies.

I said I want us to be a couple if that's ok with you. Ashley said I want us to be a couple too. She held my hand as we walked. I looked at her and we smiled at each other.

I said oh shit, Ashley said what's wrong. I said there is Amanda and her boyfriend Brad. I said I still don't understand why she would ask me to become her boyfriend when we both know that she has a boyfriend.

Ashley said she wanted a cock upgrade and I laughed out loud. She saw you on the video satisfying me thoroughly and wanted the same treatment. I said hell will freeze over before I sleep with her after releasing our sex tape.

Ashley said let's go say hello. I said why, Ashley said let's show that bitch that we are together. I said okay but this is a bad idea. We walked up to Amanda and said hello. Her boyfriend Brad said hi to me with a fist bump.

Ashley hugged Amanda and said hello. Amanda said so you two are together now. Ashley said fuck yeah, he thoroughly satisfies me in every way a man should. Amanda's eyes doubled in size. Brad said I saw your sex tape bro very impressive and he fist bumped me and Ashley.

I said thanks bro and Ashley said thanks bro. Amanda looked pissed as shit. We said later and left them. We both heard Amanda yell at her boyfriend Brad about congratulating us on the sex tape. Ashley was laughing her ass off. I smiled at her and said your enjoying this aren't you. Ashley said fuck yeah. We went back home, we hugged and kissed goodbye.

I said Amber I'm back from my walk with Ashley. Amber came out and hugged me then said dinner is ready. We ate and went to bed. The following Monday at school, Ashley and I held hands and walked through the hallways of our prep school before we went our separate ways to classes.

While we were walking, I saw girls smiling at me, I know some of them watched my sex tape. I went home later and Amber said I should invite Ashley over for dinner. I said ok, I texted Ashley that Amber wanted to invite her over for dinner. Ashley said sure and I told her when.

The night of the dinner, Amber wore a sexy little black dress that showed off her sexy curves. When the doorbell rang, it was Ashley, we hugged and kissed then she hugged Amber then said thanks for inviting me over for dinner.

It was the weekend and we were all relaxed. We sat and ate dinner talking like normal, about school, Amber's work at her nonprofit company. Amber didn't need to work; she has a shitload of money from her inheritance.

After dinner, Amber said if you guys want to be alone, you can go to his room. I said later Amber, I took Ashley by the hand and we went to my bedroom.

We reached my bedroom and I said ladies first opening the door. Ashley walked in and said wow too neat for a boy's room. I said that's not me, Amber is a neat freak, that is the only reason that it is so tidy. Ashley laughed and I said I try but Amber makes sure by checking every day.

I showed Ashley my walking closet and she said oh my god you have more clothes than I do. I said Amber is a fashionista and loves to have all the latest fashion. I don't complain because I'm not paying for it.

Ashley kissed and hugged me then said I'm very happy to be your girlfriend. I said I'm very happy to be your boyfriend. Ashley said when we were walking down the hall in school holding hands. I notice all the girls looking at you and smiling there wasn't a dry panty in the hallway.

I said I noticed all the guys checking out my hot girlfriend as we walked through the hallways holding hands there wasn't a soft dick in the hallway. Ashley laughed and said I'm proud of my curves. I said me too hot Ashley. She had the biggest smile on her pretty face.

Ashley went over my room with a fine-tooth comb. She approved of my room and said can I spend the night here. I already cleared it with my mother. I said sure, let's go clear it with my white mommy.

We went to look for Amber, we looked in the kitchen and the living room, they were both empty. I said she must be in her bedroom. I led Ashley towards Amber's bedroom, we both heard moaning. I said what the hell is that, the door was open.

We walked in and oh my god, Amber's sweet white thighs were spread wide with her finger in her pussy working hard. Her head was back, mouth was wide open moaning, she was in the throes of a powerful orgasm. Amber moaned oh god that was a big one.

When Amber opened her pretty blue eyes, she saw us both looking at her. She said oh crap sorry guys, I got horny and got a little carried away.

I was hard as a rock. Ashley noticed by rubbing my cock. She said this turns you on doesn't it seeing your hot white mommy fingering her white vagina. I said sorry Ashley but my white mommy is a hot white girl.

Ashley said you want to fuck her don't you. I said what, no. Ashley said I know you want to stick your big black cock inside of Amber's warm vagina and make her cream your cock before you cream her.

I said sorry Ashley that I'm hot for my white mommy Amber. Ashley said its ok, I don't mind if you fuck your white mommy. I said you don't mind, really. Ashley said I don't then she pulled down my pants revealing my black cock to Amber.

Amber said fuck me I want that big black penis inside my white vagina. Ashley said she wants your big cock. I walked over to the bed and crawled between Amber's sweet white thighs holding my cock.

Amber said fuck me sweetheart, I want you as bad as you want me. I held Amber's hips and forcefully entered her pussy as Ashley watched smiling at both of us. I kissed Amber as she held me tight. I pumped her white cunt full of black meat. Amber moaned with pleasure as I gave it to her very hard.

She said oh my god sweetheart, you are so good to your white mommy. I felt her orgasm as she squeezed my cock with her vagina lubricating my cock with her pussy cream.

I said it feels so amazing to be in you, Amber. She said it feels even better to receive your big black pole. I bent Amber over smacked her fat ass and fucked her even harder pulling her blonde hair as I took her violently. She rewarded my cock with another coat of cream.

Ashley said you like that big black cock don't you, Amber. Amber said oh god yeah as she came again. I gave her more cock as my orgasm released its pleasure all over my body. I moaned oh Amber as I filled her with my warm sperm.

Ashley said oh my god forbidden passions gets me every time. She kissed me passionately as I was still inside of Amber.

I laid in the middle of Amber and Ashley. Ashley said I have a confession, I showed Amber the recording of us fucking at the party. Amber was mesmerized by your big black cock, so I told her I'd be ok with you fucking her tight little cunt.

I said oh my god really. Amber said sorry we deceived you but I wanted you to penetrate and ejaculate inside of me very badly.

Ashley stroked my cock and said oh yeah, a dirty cock fresh from a warm cunt. I said you better stop that I'm going to get hard again. Ashley said I don't mind your hard cock.

Moments later, I became hard again and Amber said its hard again wow and he just fucked me. I warned you hot Ashley and you didn't stop.

Ashley said I've always wanted a dirty cock now is my only chance. She straddled me and slid her wet pussy down my dirty cock. She moaned oh god yeah that's the spot as she rode me with vigor.

I squeezed her big fucking titties as she fucked my hard cock. Amber said oh yeah Ashley ride that dirty big black cock fresh out of my cunt.

Ashley moaned and said I love your black son's big fucking cock. I felt the lubrication from Ashley's pussy. Amber said first cream, now bend over and take it like I did.

Ashley happily bent over and I penetrated her again. I pulled her hair and fucked her hard. Amber smacked her ass and Ashley creamed my cock. I moaned oh god yeah cream that fucking dick. I fucked Ashley harder and harder. I felt that wonderful tingle in my balls and I released all of my sperm into my hot ass girlfriend.

Ashley moaned and said this is the best doubleheader ever, two little white cunts fill with warm sperm from a black stud. I smiled as I lay between my favorite ladies.

Amber kissed me and said well done my black son depositing your sperm inside of our white vaginas.

Ashley kissed me and said how does it feel to fill up two

little cunts with sperm from your big black cock. I said it feels sublime to have a threesome with my hot white girlfriend and my hot white mommy.

The end

www.ingramcontent.com/pod-product-compliance
Lightning Source LLC
LaVergne TN
LVHW020538160826
845677LV00015B/4133

* 9 7 9 8 8 4 4 2 4 5 7 0 1 *